For Phillip

First published in the United States 1992 by
Dial Books for Young Readers
A Division of Penguin Books USA Inc.
375 Hudson Street
New York, New York 10014

Published in Great Britain 1991 by
The Bodley Head Children's Books,
an imprint of The Random Century Group Ltd

Printed in Hong Kong
First Edition
1 3 5 7 9 10 8 6 4 2

Library of Congress Cataloging in Publication Data
Rikys, Bodel. Red Bear / Bodel Rikys.
p.   cm.
Summary: Red Bear dresses, feeds the cat, and heads
outside for a day of fun. The names of the colors
are given on each page.
ISBN 0-8037-1048-8
[1. Bears—Fiction. 2. Color—Fiction.] I. Title.
PZ7.R448Re 1992 [E]—dc20 91-9039 CIP AC

The full-color artwork was prepared using oil pastels,
with the line drawn in brush and India ink.

Red Bear

Bodel Rikys

New York  Dial Books for Young Readers

red

yellow

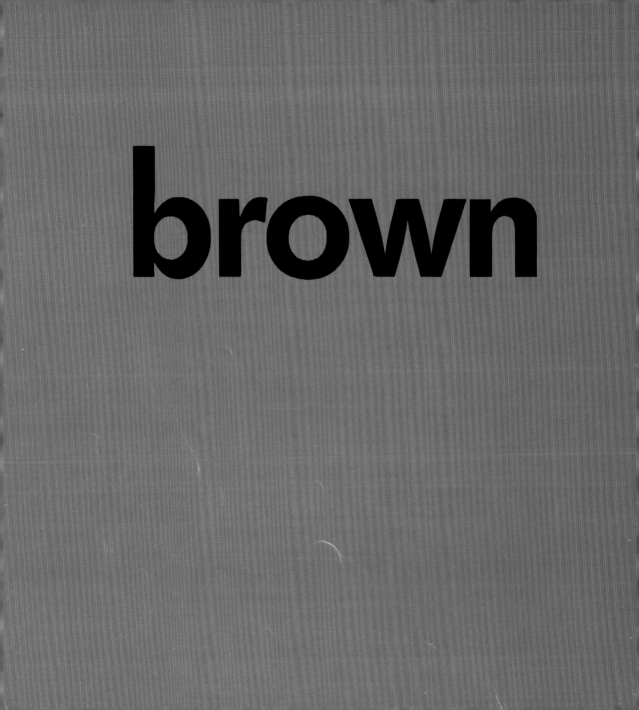

white

green

gray